The Not-So-Wicked Stepmother

By Lizi Boyd

Viking Kestrel

For Annalise and Daniel

VIKING KESTREL
Viking Penguin Inc., 40 West 23rd Street, New York, New York 10010, U.S.A.
Penguin Books Ltd, Harmondsworth, Middlesex, England
Penguin Books Australia Ltd, Ringwood, Victoria, Australia
Penguin Books Canada Limited, 2801 John Street, Markham, Ontario, Canada L3R 1B4
Penguin Books (N.Z.) Ltd, 182-190 Wairau Road, Auckland 10, New Zealand

First published in 1987 by Viking Penguin Inc.
Published simultaneously in Canada
Printed in the United States of America
Manufactured by Lake Book Cuneo, Melrose Park, Illinois
Set in Stymie Medium
1 2 3 4 5 91 90 89 88 87

Library of Congress Cataloging in Publication Data
Boyd, Lizi. The not-so-wicked stepmother.
Summary: Expecting her new stepmother to be mean,
ugly, and horrible, Hessie is surprised and confused
to find her not wicked at all.
[1. Stepmothers—Fiction] I. Title.
PZ7.B6924No 1987 [E] 86-26737 ISBN 0-670-81589-6

Hessie knew there were two kinds of wishes. Possible ones like her new red birthday bike, and impossible ones.

After her Daddy and Mommy were divorced, there was one wish she made over and over again. She would close her eyes, hold her breath, and wish her Daddy and Mommy would marry each other again.

But Hessie knew this wish was one of the impossible ones. Daddy had moved far away. Now he had married someone named Molly, whom Hessie had seen only in photographs. They lived in a little house on a lake.

Hessie was leaving tomorrow to stay with her Daddy for the summer. When her Mommy packed her suitcase, Hessie went into the bathroom. She stood in front of the mirror and made one horrible face, then another.

She whispered to herself, "I have read about stepmothers in my books. They are wicked, mean, and *VERY* ugly. They wear wrinkled black dresses, and their houses are dark and cold and dirty. The furniture is crooked and bumpy and awful. Stepdaughters have to stay inside and sweep and scrub and clean. I know she'll be horrible to me. So I'll be horrible to her!"

The next day, Hessie's Daddy came to pick her up. She was very happy to see him. He gave her a big hug and said, "We're going to have a great summer. You're going to like Molly a lot!"

"Sure," thought Hessie. "He said I'd like brussels sprouts, too. But I didn't!"

Then Hessie and her Daddy climbed into the car and drove all day to get to the lake. Finally they came to a long, bumpy driveway. At the end was a house with a big porch over the lake. The sun was shining down everywhere. "That was a *VERY* dark, bumpy driveway," thought Hessie, "but it is a pretty house."

Hessie saw Molly working in a big flower garden. She was wearing a bright-colored dress. She waved to Hessie. Then Molly came down to say hello. Hessie said hello, too, and then she made one of her horrible faces. No one noticed.

That evening when they sat down to dinner, Hessie thought to herself, "This food may be poison and it doesn't smell like anything my Mommy cooks. I'm not going to eat it!" And she didn't! But no one said anything.

Later, when Hessie climbed into her bed, she whispered, "I know it will be hard," and it did feel different and smell different, but it was comfortable.

Daddy read Hessie a story and then turned out the lights. Above the bed was a big skylight, and outside the fireflies blinked and the stars twinkled.

"This is just a trick!" thought Hessie, and then she fell asleep.

Next morning, Daddy made Hessie her favorite breakfast of toast and jam and eggs. Then Molly came into the kitchen with two buckets. "Ahh! Now the mean stepmother is going to make me scrub the floor!" But instead Molly said, "This is duck food. Would you like to feed the ducks?"

After Hessie fed the ducks they all put on their bathing suits and went down to the beach below the porch.

Hessie and her Daddy played while Molly swam far out into the lake. "Good," thought Hessie, "maybe she can't swim back and Daddy and I can live here alone!"

Just at that moment all the ducks swam by Molly. Hessie closed her eyes, held her breath, and wished she could swim far out into the lake like Molly and the ducks.

Hessie was confused. "Stepdaughters are not supposed to like their stepmothers," she thought. "She isn't as pretty as Mommy, but she isn't ugly and she hasn't been mean to me. Somewhere she must be hiding her ugly-stepmother clothes and her long, pointed black shoes. I will sneak around and look for stepmother clues!"

So Hessie snooped in the bathroom. She tried Molly's perfume. It smelled good.

She looked under the bed, and there was a big black trunk. "Ah ha!" thought Hessie. "I've found it!" But just then Molly came into the room and said, "Oh, you've found my old trunk of clothes. Do you want to play dress-up?"

The trunk was filled with colorful dresses! Scarves, a fluffy boa, necklaces and bracelets, and finally a pair of shiny black pointed shoes, but too tiny for a witch.

Hessie dressed up and looked into the mirror. "Oh, how pretty you look," she said to her reflection. "Where are you going tonight?" Then Hessie remembered to make her horrible face.

But Hessie began to forget to make her horrible faces. She couldn't make them when she was swimming or when she ate or if she was talking or laughing. And besides, nobody ever seemed to notice. Feeding the ducks made Hessie smile. She liked this house on the lake. She loved her bed under the stars.

On Monday, Daddy went to work. Hessie thought, "Now maybe Molly will be the mean stepmother." But instead Molly said, "I want to take you to a special place." So they made a picnic lunch. And walked through the woods until they came to a clearing with high blueberry bushes all around. They ate their lunch. "Let's pick blueberries for Daddy!" Hessie and Molly filled the empty basket.

The sun grew hotter. Hessie said, "Let's go swimming. Molly, will you teach me? I want to swim like you, far out into the lake."

First Molly taught Hessie to blow bubbles. Then to float and kick. Hessie was learning to swim! "My wish will come true," thought Hessie. "I will swim with the ducks!"

Next day, after they'd gone swimming, Molly said to Hessie, "I'm going to wash my hair in the shower. Do you want to wash yours, too?" "Sure," said Hessie. "This shower looks like fun!" So Molly and Hessie climbed into the shower and soaped up their hair. Suddenly Hessie felt a stinging in her eyes. She began to cry and scream. "Mommy never washes my hair in the shower! You hurt me! I think you are wicked and mean!"

Hessie cried and screamed until her Daddy came home. She really missed her Mommy now, and that's why she was still crying. But she didn't tell that to Molly or her Daddy.

Hessie was still sad the next day. "Do you want to call your Mommy?" her Daddy asked. Her Mommy's voice made Hessie feel warm and happy. "Molly is teaching me to swim. I have ten ducks to feed every morning. We have a canoe, and I have a big bed underneath a big window. But I miss you, Mommy." Hessie's Mommy said, "I can't wait to see you swim! It sounds like you're having fun. Big kisses, Hessie. I love you. See you soon."

Hessie hung up. She stopped being sad. But she noticed that Molly was quiet and seemed unhappy. Hessie gave her a big hug to cheer her up. She said, "Come with me, Molly. Let's pick flowers."

That night, they paddled the canoe to a little island in the middle of the lake. They built a fire and cooked their dinner. They all slept outside under the stars.

Soon it was Molly's birthday. Hessie and her Daddy baked her a surprise cake. It was *VERY* bumpy and crooked, but it was full of chocolate. Molly loved it and said it tasted very, very good.

It was the night before Hessie was going home. Daddy and Molly climbed into Hessie's bed. They all took turns telling stories. Molly made up a story about three ducks: Daddy-man Duck, Hess-a-bless Duck, and Molly-moo Duck. The ducks lived on a lake and spent their summer swimming around in the clear blue water. A little girl lived on the lake, too. She fed them delicious pieces of bread and corn. When the summer was over, the little girl went home to her Mommy. And then it was time for the ducks to fly south for the winter. Every summer the ducks came back, and so did the little girl.

Hessie and Daddy and Molly all lay in bed quacking and laughing and pretending to be ducks. Then they turned out the lights and watched the blinking fireflies and shiny stars above Hessie's bed.

"Goodbye, bed," Hessie said in the morning. "Goodbye, lake and ducks and house. I'll see you next summer." Then Hessie and Daddy and Molly gave each other great big goodbye hugs.